RUSS THOMPSON

ELECTRO BLAST

Finding Forward

Books

Published by Finding Forward Books.
P.O. Box 8182, Long Beach, California 90808.
www.findingforwardbooks.com

Editing by Laura Perkins. Series concept by Pam Sheppard. Text set in Open Dyslexic Mono. Cover photo by Shutterstock.

Library of Congress Control Number 2025926456
ISBN 979-1-964809-09-0 (Ingram paperback)
ISBN 979-8-241740-73-1 (Amazon paperback)
ASIN B0GCYCCLLS (Amazon Kindle)
FILE FF014-23A-20260102

Summary: A shy tenth grader finds success when he joins the school jazz band.

BISAC Subject Codes: | YOUNG ADULT FICTION / Social Themes / Emotions and Feelings | YOUNG ADULT FICTION / Social Themes / Self-Esteem

***

For Betty Jean,
our kids,
and grandkids.

CONTENTS

1 MAYBE IT WILL

FRIDAY MORNING, October 13. Not a lucky day.

Mom and I enter the main building of Edison High School and walk down the hall.

I try not to be nervous. But I feel all the kids looking at me.

"Angelo, it's going to be okay," Mom says. "This will be a fresh start for you."

I hate this place. I don't know anybody here.

We step into the counseling

office. Mom gives my paperwork to the lady at the front counter.

Minutes pass. Another lady comes out and calls us into her office.

"Angelo, I'm Ms. Boyle," she says. "Welcome to Edison High School."

She's old, about forty, wearing a blue sweater with a hole in the sleeve.

Mom and I sit down across from her. She types into her computer and looks up at us.

"Angelo, I put you into all the required courses for tenth graders," she says. "You have English 10, physical science, health, P.E., and geometry."

They're the same classes I had at Franklin High School. I hope they go better here.

"You also have to take a fine-arts course," Ms. Boyle says. "We have room in beginning band. What do you think?"

"Do you have any drawing classes or ceramics?"

"They're all closed," she says. "But we do have art history."

"That's okay," I say. "I'll take band."

Ms. Boyle prints out my class schedule. "Welcome to Edison High School."

She smiles like she really means it.

Maybe it will be okay here.

2 SAFE

THE BELL RINGS. Kids pour into the hallway.

They're smiling and laughing, like school is fun for them.

School has never been fun for me.

I look at my class schedule. I have geometry in room 117.

Where is it?

I follow the hall and turn right.

Kids are walking everywhere. They know where they're going.

I can't find my classroom.

Minutes pass.

The hall is almost empty.

I look at the map Ms. Boyle gave me.

The bell rings.

I'm tardy now.

I see the door to my geometry classroom.

But I don't go in.

Everyone is going to look at me if I walk in late.

I leave the building, turn left, and see the lunch area.

It's empty.

I pass through the food court, turn the corner, and sit against the wall where nobody will see me.

I close my eyes and feel the sun on my face.

I know I shouldn't do this.

But I feel safe here.

3 HATE THIS PLACE

I LOOK UP. A lady wearing a security jacket stands in front of me.

"What are you doing?" she asks.

"Nothing."

"I can see that," she says. "How come I don't know you?"

"It's my first day here. I couldn't find my classroom."

"Interesting," she says. "How come you didn't ask for help?"

"I don't know."

"What's your name?" she asks.

"Angelo Pruitt."

"Come with me," she says. "We're
going to the guidance room."

"What's that?"

"It's a place where you will
write a paper about how to do better
in school."

I get up and walk next to her.

I'm all alone here.

I hate this place.

4 OLD SCHOOL

GUIDANCE ROOM. It's a big classroom with about thirty desks. A few kids are sitting and writing.

I go to the lady at the front. She looks old, like she could be somebody's grandma. She hands me a piece of paper.

"This is the form for your Edison Excellence Essay," she says. "The directions are to explain what you did wrong and how you will do better next time. Be sure to write neatly."

We never had anything like this

at Franklin High School.

They just yelled at us and told us to quit messing up.

I find a seat that's far away from everybody and begin writing.

EDISON EXCELLENCE ESSAY

Angelo Pruitt
Grade 10

It's my first day here at Edison High School.

I wanted to have a nice day and get off to a good start.

But I couldn't find my geometry classroom. And I couldn't just go up to someone I didn't know and ask for help.

Then the bell rang. I didn't know where to go, so I sat down behind the food court.

I know how to be successful in school.

You have to go every day, listen to the teachers, and work hard. You also have to ask questions if you don't understand.

Before this I went to Franklin High School. I was there all last year and the beginning of this year.

It was good because I knew the people there. And they knew me.

But at this school I don't know anybody.

I don't feel comfortable here. There is nobody I know at all.

I wish I was still at Franklin.

But we had to move to Conroy because my mom got a new job.

She's the night manager at Price Mart.

It pays more than her other job.
And we have a bigger apartment now.
    But I liked it better at my old
school.

5 LOOKING AT ME

I FINISH WRITING. A big man wearing a tie comes to my desk. He looks like he used to play football.

"Angelo, my name is Mr. Wiley," he says. "I'm one of the deans. Can I see what you wrote?"

I give him my paper. He sits in the chair next to me and reads.

"It looks like you had a tough morning," he says. "One thing I want you to know is that there are people here who will help you. All you need to do is ask."

It's nice of him to say that. I should have asked for directions.

"You also need to know that we are very strict on discipline here," he says. "Your essay will be scanned and added to your school records. Your parent will also be notified. Don't mess up again."

I want to say something back. But it would just cause problems.

I wasn't trying to mess up.

I just didn't want to walk into my class late and have the other kids looking at me.

6 LIKE A FOOL

HOME. Mom is working late tonight. I'm all alone.

I get a frozen dinner out of the refrigerator, put it in the microwave, and set the timer.

I hate eating by myself. But that's the way it is now.

I turn on the news. A story comes on about a kid who helped another kid who was being bullied at school.

I remember what happened to me at Franklin.

It was not good.

The teacher called on me to read
out loud in my history class.

At first, I was doing okay.

But I got nervous and messed up
on one of the words.

Then I started messing up on all
the words.

Nobody said anything.

But they all looked at me like I
was stupid.

I had to sit there like a fool
and act like it didn't bother me.

7 WISH I KNEW

TEN O'CLOCK. I lie in bed playing Sky Power.

The front door opens. It's Mom.

I turn off the game and roll over to pretend I'm sleeping.

My bedroom door opens. The lights go on.

"Angelo, I don't care if you are asleep," she says. "You need to sit up now so I can talk to you. This is no joke."

I sit up and rub my eyes to make her think I was sleeping.

"You lied to me," she says. "You told me you were going to try hard at Edison."

"I tried to find my class. But the bell rang. I didn't know where to go."

"Mr. Wiley called me," she says. "I also read the essay you wrote. What is your problem?"

I look at her, but I don't know what to say.

"Something is going on with you," she says. "First, you mess up at Franklin. Then you get a fresh start at Edison, and you mess that up, too."

She wants to know what my problem is.

I wish I knew.

8 JUST SAY YES

MONDAY. Edison High School. The bell rings to go to second period. I walk to my geometry class.

The teacher is a tall lady with a gray streak in her hair. She smiles when I show her my class schedule.

"Angelo, are you new to Edison or just this class?" she asks.

"I'm new to Edison."

"I'm Ms. Rico," she says. "Welcome to geometry."

She points to a desk in the middle.

I take my seat, open my laptop, and look around the room.

The girl next to me smiles. She seems like she might be nice.

But I pretend not to notice her.

The bell rings to begin class. Ms. Rico comes to the front.

"We have a new student," she says. "Please give a welcome to Angelo Pruitt."

I wish she hadn't said that. I don't like to stand out.

Then they clap for me.

That makes it worse.

"Open your laptops and get on the Khan Academy," Ms. Rico says. "Go to Unit 2, Finding Measures. Discuss it with your elbow partner after you watch the video."

I find the Khan Academy. But I can't find Unit 2.

The girl next to me smiles again.

"I can help you," she says.

She's trying to be nice.

But I don't answer.

Minutes pass. I still can't find Unit 2.

"Are you sure I can't help you?" she asks.

I go back to the home page and try again.

But I still can't find the unit.

Why can't I just say yes?

9 GOOD CLASS

BAND. Second period. Mr. Haney comes to the front. He's a young guy with spikey hair and a bow tie.

I show him my class schedule.

"Angelo, glad to have you," he says. "Anything you want to play?"

"Clarinet?" I ask.

He shakes his head. "Anything else?"

"Saxophone?"

He shakes his head again. "We need somebody on the trombone. Are you up for it?"

I don't know anything about the trombone. But I have to play something.

"Okay," I say.

Mr. Haney signs my class schedule. "Everyone is learning together in here," he says. "The band room is open every day during lunch. You can come and practice as much as you want."

The next thing I know, I'm sitting in the back with a trombone in my hands.

The guy next to me also has a trombone. He's wearing a faded flannel shirt with a torn sleeve. He reaches out to shake my hand.

"I'm Sully," he says.

I shake back.

"I'm Angelo."

Mr. Haney comes to the front.

"Everybody, give a welcome to Angelo Pruitt," he says. "You know what to do."

His baton goes up.

They raise their instruments.

His baton goes down.

They blow into their horns.

It's a loud blast that's pure noise.

"That was the Edison *Electro Blast*," Sully says. "We do it for Thomas Edison."

I'm in the band now.

They're trying to be nice.

Maybe this will be a good class.

10 DIDN'T KNOW

TUESDAY MORNING. Breakfast. I sit at the kitchen table and pour a bowl of cereal.

Mom's door opens. She comes into the kitchen and sits across from me. She probably wants to talk.

"Angelo, how was school yesterday?" she asks.

"It was okay."

"How were your classes?"

"They were fine."

"What about your teachers?"

"They were fine, too."

"Anything else?" she asks.

"Nothing," I say. "Everything was fine."

She seems okay when she gets up to make a cup of coffee.

But when she comes back to the table, something is wrong.

"I love you," she says. "And I care about what happens to you. But whenever I try to talk with you, I get the silent treatment."

I see the look in her eyes.

A tear goes down her cheek.

I didn't know I was hurting her.

11 DON'T CARE

EDISON HIGH SCHOOL. Geometry. It's my second day here.

Ms. Rico comes to the front of the classroom.

"I want to go over what we did yesterday," she says. "Get on the Khan Academy and go to Unit 2, Finding Measures."

I worked on it last night, so I know how to find the unit.

But I don't understand how to do the work.

It's stupid.

I don't care about measuring
lines.

I don't care about measuring
angles.

And I don't care about this
class.

12 MAYBE I CAN

BAND CLASS. Mr. Haney smiles when I
get to the door.

He acts like he's glad to see me.

Maybe things will really be okay
in here.

I get my trombone from the shelf
and sit in the back next to Sully.

Everyone is playing notes to warm
up.

I blow into my trombone, but no
sound comes out.

"Watch me," Sully says.

He shows me how to push my lips

together and buzz into the
mouthpiece.

I try it. A sound comes out.

Mr. Haney comes to the front.
"Band, let's blast," he says.

His baton goes up.

We raise our instruments.

His baton goes down.

I blow into my trombone as loud
as I can just like everybody else.

It's pure noise.

It's the Edison *Electro Blast*.

I feel like I belong.

Class is almost over when Mr.
Haney calls me to his desk.

He gives me a mouthpiece and a
book that says, *Beginning Trombone*.

"Angelo, I don't have a trombone
to check out to you," he says. "But
this book will give you some tips on
getting started. You can also blow

into the mouthpiece at home to learn how to make sounds. If you work hard, I think you have a chance to be really good."

From the way he says it, I think he believes it.

Maybe I can get good.

13 A WAY

AFTER DINNER. I get on my laptop to begin my geometry homework.

But I just can't think.

I turn on the TV and pick up the controller to play Sky Power.

Planes fly everywhere. I shoot down a lot of them. But it doesn't seem fun today.

I think about band class and how Mr. Haney said I could be good.

I get the mouthpiece he gave me and look at the book on playing the trombone.

I also get on YouTube and type *beginning trombone* into the search box.

It shows a seven-year-old kid playing *Happy Birthday* on his trombone.

If he can do it, I can do it too.

I play along on the mouthpiece. Each time I play it, I sound better.

That's when it hits me. I wonder how much it costs to buy a trombone.

I get on my computer. There's a plastic one on the Price Mart website for $199.

That's a lot of money.

But maybe there's a way.

14 GO THERE

WEDNESDAY MORNING. Breakfast. I pour a bowl of cereal and begin eating.

I think about my homework for geometry.

I tried to do it last night. But it was just too hard.

Mom sits down across from me with a cup of coffee. She has a look on her face like she's worn out.

"How was work last night?" I ask.

"We got a late shipment from the warehouse," she says. "It took a long time until everything got put away."

She takes another sip of coffee. I wish she didn't have to work so hard.

"How was school yesterday?" she asks.

"I think I'm going to like my band class. Mr. Haney gave me a book on how to play the trombone. He also gave me a mouthpiece so I can practice making sounds."

"That's interesting," she says.

"I also found a plastic trombone on the Price Mart website for $199."

"That's a lot of money," she says.

"I know it's a lot. But it's a lot cheaper than a brass one. I was wondering if you could lend me the money, and I could get a job to pay you back."

She looks at me like she's thinking.

"We can do that," she says. "But I don't want you working during the week. Also, you need to talk to your teacher and get his opinion on buying a plastic trombone. I don't want you getting something that won't be good."

I think about a restaurant we drove by on Sunday. The name of it was Golden Grill. They had a Help Wanted sign in the window.

Maybe I can go there after school today.

15 WALK OUT

AFTER SCHOOL. I stand outside the door of Golden Grill.

The Help Wanted sign still hangs in the window.

I get ready to go in.

But they probably won't want me.

I turn to walk away.

But I told Mom I would apply.

I turn back and go inside.

The hostess smiles and seems nice. "Can I help you?" she asks.

I try to keep my voice steady. "Do you still have a job opening?"

She smiles again and gives me an application.

I sit down and begin writing. I try my best. But I make mistakes and have to cross them out.

She thanks me when I give her the application and takes it to the back.

I should walk out. I know I'm not going to get the job.

The manager comes out and shakes my hand. He has a strong grip.

"Angelo, nice to meet you," he says. "Come with me."

I follow him through the kitchen to a cramped office.

I wish this was over. I don't feel good.

"I need a dishwasher and someone to bus tables," he says. "You have to show up on time, follow instructions, and work hard. I need someone I can depend on."

I look around the office.

I try to say something.

But the words don't come out.

"Where do you go to school?" he asks.

"I just started at Edison."

"Where were you before that?"

"Franklin."

"Can I see your grades?" he asks.

I don't have a choice. I have to do it.

I pull out my phone and get ready to show him.

But I have a NoPass and two D's.

There's no way he's going to hire me.

I put away my phone and walk out.

16 GOOD GRADES

HOME. I feel better when I open the door and step inside.

But I also feel bad.

I shouldn't have walked out of Golden Grill.

The manager was trying to be nice.

Maybe my grades would have been no big deal.

I turn on the TV and get on Sky Power.

It feels good to shoot the planes down.

Twenty minutes pass.

I should start on my homework.

But I'm only going to play for a little while longer.

I blast more planes out of the sky.

Then I think about school.

I messed up at Franklin. But Edison is a fresh start for me.

My only hard class is geometry.

I know I can do better if I work harder.

I'm going to quit playing around, do my work, and get good grades.

17 SAY NO

THURSDAY MORNING. Breakfast. I pour a bowl of cereal. Mom sits across from me.

"Angelo, what happened at the restaurant yesterday?" she asks.

I don't want to lie. But I don't know what else to say.

"I went there and saw the manager. The job was already taken."

"Try not to be discouraged," she says. "I know there's a job out there for you."

I feel worse now.

But how could I tell her what really happened?

And he wasn't going to hire me, anyway.

I think about asking if she can still lend me the money to buy a trombone.

But she will probably just say no.

18 LOT OF WORK

SATURDAY MORNING. I sit on the steps
outside our apartment.

The sun is out. It's going to be
a warm day.

I look down at the courtyard. The
manager of the apartments is
carrying some buckets of paint. He's
always doing something.

"Mr. Toliver," I ask. "Can you
use some help?"

"Angelo, that would be great," he
says.

I walk down the stairs and go

with him to an empty apartment. It's
clean, but the walls need painting.

"I have to get it ready to rent
out again," Mr. Toliver says. "The
other guy who was working for me
quit."

He looks at me like he's thinking
about something.

"The job pays minimum wage," he
says. "I need somebody I can depend
on who can work every Saturday. Are
you up for it?"

"You bet!"

"Go home and put on some old
clothes," he says. "We have a lot of
work to do."

19 WE CAN ORDER

KITCHEN. Six o'clock. Mom is home early tonight.

I take our dinners out of the microwave and put them on the table.

I think about the paycheck I got today. It makes me feel good, like I earned something.

We begin eating.

"Angelo, it's nice to see you smiling," Mom says. "How was your day?"

"I got a job."

Her face lights up. "Where at?"

"I'm working every Saturday for Mr. Toliver. I helped him paint an apartment today."

"I'm so proud of you," she says. "This is a big day. I guess we can order your trombone after dinner."

20 WORK HARD

TUESDAY. After school. I run up the stairs to our apartment. Mom texted me that the trombone came.

The box is on the kitchen table. I put it together and buzz into the mouthpiece.

It plays.

And It doesn't sound like plastic. It sounds just as good as the one I have at school.

I get out my music book and play *London Bridge Is Falling Down*.

The guy next door starts banging

on the wall.

I go into the closet, close the door, and play again.

No more pounding.

I'll be able to practice at home as much as I want.

I'm going to work hard and get really good.

21 HAVE TO PASS

WEDNESDAY. Period two. I take my seat in geometry.

I didn't do my homework last night because I was playing my new trombone.

But I'll make sure I get it done tonight.

The bell rings.

Ms. Rico comes to the front.

"I know that geometry is hard," she says. "It was a tough class for me when I was in school, so I know what some of you are going through."

It surprises me to hear her say that. I thought geometry would have been easy for her.

"The thing I want you to know is that if you work hard and try your best, sooner or later you will get it."

She turns and starts drawing a bunch of triangles on the board with letters on the sides.

She wants us to figure out the size of the angles and how long the sides are.

But I don't like it.

And I never will.

I wish I could take something else.

But I don't have a choice.

I have to pass this class in order to graduate.

22 I'M GOING

PERIOD THREE. I walk to band class. Mr. Haney stands at the door.

"Angelo, how are you doing?" he asks.

"I got the trombone I was telling you about, the plastic one."

"That is so great," he says. "You are on your way."

I sit in the back next to Sully and wait for class to start.

The bell rings. Mr. Haney comes to the front.

"If any of you are interested,"

we're forming a jazz band," he says.
"It's called the Electros. You'll be
playing at our basketball games and
other events. Practice will be every
day after school, beginning next
Monday. It doesn't matter how good
you are. It's open to everybody."

I look at Sully.

He smiles and nods his head.

I'm not very good yet.

But I'm going to join, too.

23 LOT TO DO

MONDAY. After school. I get to the band room and sit next to Sully.

I've been practicing a lot at home. I'm excited about being on the Electros.

Mr. Haney comes to the front. "The nice thing about the Electros is that you are going to become good players," he says. "But it will not be easy. You will have to put in a lot of work."

I look around the room. We have two guys playing trumpets, a girl playing clarinet, a girl on the drums, and Sully and me playing trombone.

"Let's get started," Mr. Haney says. "We have a lot to do."

24 HAVEN'T STUDIED

FIVE WEEKS LATER. Wednesday afternoon, basketball gym. I sit in the bleachers next to Sully.

We're wearing our Edison Electro shirts.

I'm nervous. But I've been practicing at home for almost two hours every night. I know all the songs by heart.

Maricela, our band leader, stands at the front and faces us. Her baton goes up.

We raise our instruments.

Her baton goes down.

We play the *Edison Fight Song*.

The players run out and start shooting baskets.

The cheerleaders start dancing on the basketball floor.

The crowd cheers.

I feel great.

Then it hits me.

We have a test in geometry tomorrow.

I haven't studied yet.

25 STILL DON'T

THURSDAY. Geometry. Ms. Rico comes to the front of the classroom with our test papers.

"You will get forty minutes," she says. "Show your work and write neatly. Keep your eyes on your own paper."

She passes out the tests and says to begin.

I get a bad feeling.

I know how to do the first three problems.

But I'm not sure about the rest.

I studied late last night when I got home from the basketball game.

I also got up early and studied this morning.

But I still don't know it.

26 SHOULD BE

FRIDAY. Geometry. Ms. Rico comes to the front.

"I'm going to pass back your tests from yesterday," she says. "Most of you did well. But some of you had trouble. I can help you if you come after school. Don't put it off if you're having a hard time."

I get my paper. It's a D.

I know I should go in to see Ms. Rico after school.

But I have to go to practice for the Electros.

Ms. Rico finishes handing back our papers.

She spends the rest of class going over the answers to the questions.

I think I understand how to do the problems now.

I don't think I need to get help after school.

I should be okay for the next test if I study extra hard this weekend.

27 HAVE TO GET

AFTER SCHOOL. The Electros play at
the basketball game tonight.

I go to the band room to get
ready.

Mr. Haney comes to the front.

"I know you're having a good time
playing at the basketball games," he
says. "But I need to say some things
about your grades."

I knew this was coming. I don't
feel good about geometry. My other
classes are fine.

"I'll be checking your grades on

School View next week before the Jefferson game," he says. "You must have a C or higher in every class to be eligible. If you don't, you will not be able to play."

It gives me a chill to hear him say that.

I have to get a good grade on the geometry test next Wednesday.

28　GOING TO DO

SATURDAY. Six o'clock in the morning. It's still dark.

I have two hours before I go to work for Mr. Toliver.

I sit at the kitchen table, open my laptop to School View, and go to geometry.

I read the section where it explains what to do.

But it's hard.

I look again at my test from last week. I see the red checkmarks and the D at the top.

I've always been bad in math. But this is really bad.

I go to the first problem and try to figure it out again.

Ms. Rico explained it in class.

And I understood all of it.

But now that I'm at home, I don't understand any of it.

I go to the Khan Academy.

I don't understand that either.

What am I going to do?

29 NOT GOING

AFTER BREAKFAST. I walk down the stairs to work with Mr. Toliver.

We're in Apartment 10 today. We begin painting in the kitchen.

"Angelo, how are the Electros?" he asks.

"It's fun. The people in the band are cool. And we don't have to be perfect."

"How about your classes?" he asks.

"I'm doing okay in everything except geometry."

"That's a big one," he says. "Are you getting help?"

"It's hard because I have to go to band practice after school."

He stops painting and looks me in the eye.

"When it comes to your classes, don't play around," he says. "Be sure to talk to your geometry teacher. If you need help, make sure you get it."

I know he means well.

But it's not as simple as he thinks it is.

I'm not going to give up playing on the Electros.

30 BEST THING

SATURDAY NIGHT. Ten o'clock. I sit at the kitchen table. I've been working on geometry since we finished dinner.

I begin the next problem. But my mind goes blank.

Mom comes in and sits across from me. "Angelo, you need to get some sleep," she says.

"I know. But I have to get this work done. It won't be much longer."

I look at the problem again.

It doesn't help.

I keep hoping that things will click and I'll understand it.

But the harder I try, the worse it gets.

Mr. Toliver said I need to talk to Ms. Rico.

But she's going to say I need to come to her classroom after school every day.

If I do that, I'll be off the Electros.

And the Electros are the best thing that's ever happened to me.

31 TIME

TUESDAY EVENING. I sit at the kitchen table with my laptop open. Our geometry test is tomorrow.

I don't know it.

I don't know it.

I don't know it.

I read the study sheet and start the first problem again.

It doesn't make sense.

It doesn't make sense.

It doesn't make sense.

When I went to Ms. Rico after school today, she said I should have come in for help a long time ago.

She said I could learn it. But it would take time.

The test is tomorrow.

I don't have the time.

32 DON'T KNOW

WEDNESDAY. Geometry. The test is today.

I walk through the door and take my seat.

I know I'm going to fail.

The bell rings to begin class.

Ms. Rico comes to the front with our test papers.

"Clear your desks," she says. "You will get forty minutes. Work carefully. Go back and check your answers if you finish early."

She passes out the tests.

I look at the first problem.

I don't know how to do it.

I look at the next problem.

I don't know how to do that one, either.

33 EVERYTHING

AFTER SCHOOL. I go to Ms. Rico's classroom.

The door is open.

She's checking papers.

Maybe it will be good news.

I sit in the chair next to her desk.

"Angelo, I'm sorry," she says. "But you got a D on your test."

I'm afraid to ask. But I have to know. "What about my report card?"

"It will be the same," she says. "You'll be getting a D."

It's over.

I'm done.

The Electros have been everything
to me.

34 IT'S OVER

AFTER SCHOOL. I go to the band room. The Electros are practicing. Sully waves.

Mr. Haney stands behind his desk and watches them practice.

"Angelo, how did your geometry test go?" he asks.

"I got a D. I'll also be getting a D on my report card."

"I'm sorry," he says.

I know what the answer is going to be. But I decide to ask anyway.

"Is there any way you can make an

exception and let me stay on the Electros?"

"I can't do that," Mr. Haney says. "But as soon as you bring your grade up, you'll be back."

I leave the room and stand outside to listen.

I wish I was in there with them.

It's over.

35 DOESN'T KNOW

SATURDAY MORNING. I finish breakfast, walk down the stairs, and meet Mr. Toliver in his workshop.

It's hard not to think about band. I'm tired of getting beat.

"Angelo, what's wrong?" Mr. Toliver asks.

"I got put off the Electros. I got a D in geometry on my 15-week report card."

He motions for me to sit in the chair across from him.

"What will happen if you bring up

your grade?".

"I'LL be back on the Electros. But I've already tried everything."

"I know it's been hard for you," he says. "And I know you feel like quitting. But if you quit trying, you will never get better. If you keep trying, you can."

He makes it sound easy.

He doesn't know what I'm going through.

36 HAVE TO

MONDAY. After school. I take a seat in Ms. Rico's classroom. Five other students are also there.

"I'm glad you're all here," she says. "Geometry is difficult. But if you work hard, you will be successful."

I look around the classroom. The other students seem like they've been beaten down, too.

"The other thing you need to know is that the harder you work, the easier it gets," she says. "The work you put in now is going to help you in all your future math classes."

She goes to the board and shows us how to do the first problem.

I get it wrong.

I also get the second problem wrong.

It's going to be hard.

But I have to do it.

37 THINK I CAN

WEDNESDAY. Geometry. It's our first test since we came back from winter vacation.

I've been coming to Ms. Rico's classroom every day after school.

I've also been working hard at home on the Khan Academy.

It's been a lot of work. But I feel ready.

Ms. Rico comes to the front of the classroom.

"Clear your desks," she says. "You will have forty minutes. No

wandering eyes. Keep your paper
covered as you work."
     She passes out the tests.
     The questions look hard.
     But I think I can do them.

38   HATE THIS PLACE

THURSDAY. Geometry. Ms. Rico hands back our tests from yesterday.

I feel good.

I might even get a B.

But when I see my paper, it's a D.

I did all that work.

But I missed a C by three points.

She told us to keep trying and never give up.

I did everything she said.

I hate this place.

39 KEEP TRYING

THURSDAY. After school. I feel like quitting.

But I go to Ms. Rico's classroom anyway.

She comes to the front and looks at each of us.

"I know that some of you had a hard time on the test," she says. "But even if you got a bad grade, I want you to know that I'm still proud of you."

She looks straight at me. I don't feel proud of myself. I feel dumb.

"By coming here and working after school every day, you're showing persistence," she says. "No matter how bad you feel, make up your mind that you will never give up. If you have a problem and keep trying, you can fix it. But if you give up, you will never fix it."

I feel like giving up.

But if I want to play on the Electros again, I have to keep trying.

40 ALL I NEED

FOUR WEEKS LATER. Thursday night. I sit at the kitchen table. It's after ten o'clock.

I'm tired. But I have to keep going.

Our final exam in geometry is tomorrow. I need a C to get back on the Electros.

I look at the review problems on my laptop again.

I've done each one twice.

I begin doing them again to make sure I really know them.

Ms. Rico told us to keep trying and never give up.

I finish the last problem and turn off the laptop.

It's been a lot of work.

All I need is a C.

41 KNOW HOW

FRIDAY. Geometry. It's test day, our final exam.

I try to be calm.

I think about all the work I've done.

I think about the Electros.

Ms. Rico comes to the front of the classroom.

"Many of you have improved," she says. "I think you're going to do well. Relax, do your best, and good luck."

I get my test paper and look at

the problems.

I never thought this would happen
to me.

I know how to do them.

42 LEARN IT

EVENING. Kitchen. I turn off the stove and bring our food to the table. I made chicken with rice and vegetables.

Mom comes in from her room. We sit down to eat.

"Angelo, you sure are smiling," she says.

"I feel good about my geometry final. I think I'm going to get a good grade."

"I'm so relieved," she says. "You have worked so hard."

"Ms. Rico told us to keep trying.
I didn't think it would happen. But
I knew how to answer most of the
questions."

"I was worried that school was
going to bring you down again, like
it did at Franklin," she says.

"Me too," I say. "But I feel
different now. Even if it's math, I
feel like I can learn it if I work
hard."

43 DON'T FEEL

SATURDAY MORNING. I go downstairs and meet Mr. Toliver in Apartment 12.

It's a mess. I put on the rubber gloves and begin cleaning the stove.

Mr. Toliver scrubs the sink. "Angelo, you seem happy this morning. What happened?"

"We had our final exam in geometry yesterday. I think I did okay."

"What do you mean by okay?" he asks.

"I knew how to do every problem. I'll find out my grade on Monday. I'll be back on the Electros if I get a C or higher."

"What do you think happened?" he asks.

"You told me to ask for help, and I did. I also worked hard. After all this time, I don't feel dumb in geometry anymore."

44 I'M BACK

MONDAY. Band class. It's the first day of the second semester. I smile when I see Mr. Haney.

"Angelo, is it good news?" he asks.

"It's great news."

I show him my report card. I have a C in geometry.

He smiles and shakes my hand. "Welcome back!" he says.

I get my trombone and sit next to Sully. He gives me a high-five.

The bell rings to begin class.

Mr. Haney comes to the front.

"I have an announcement," he says. "Angelo is back on the Electros. You all know what to do."

His baton goes up.

We get ready to play.

His baton goes down.

We blow into our horns as loud as we can.

It's the Edison *Electro Blast*.

I'm back.

45 FUN DAY

WEDNESDAY. After school. Band room.
It's my third day back with the
Electros.

I still know all the songs
because I've been practicing at
home. I feel like I've never been
gone.

Mr. Haney comes to the front.

"I got a call from the manager of
The Conroy Retirement Home," he
says. "They're having a special
celebration for Valentine's Day.
Raise your hand if you would like to

play for them."

We all raise our hands. Everyone
smiles.

"Be here at one o'clock," Mr.
Haney says. "It's going to be a fun
day."

46 GOOD TIME

SATURDAY. CONROY RETIREMENT HOME. We go to the front of the recreation room and get ready to perform.

About thirty people are here. It feels good to see them smile.

Mr. Haney steps to the microphone. "It's our great pleasure to be with you as we get ready for Valentine's Day. Our first song will be, *You Are My Sunshine*."

We begin playing.

A man and his wife get up and start dancing.

Then a lot of them get up to
dance.

We finish and get ready for the
next song.

Sully pokes me in the ribs.

"This is cool," he says. "They're
having a good time."

47 DIDN'T PLAY

SATURDAY AFTERNOON. I'm tired when I get home. But it's a good tired.

"Angelo, you look happy," Mom says. "How was the retirement home?"

"The people were smiling and tapping their feet. Some of them got up and started dancing."

"I think you did something nice today," she says.

I remember how it was in September.

Everything was bad. And I hated school.

But things are different now.

I'm getting good grades. And school is better.

It felt good to see those people smile today.

And I didn't play any bad notes.

48 ELECTRO BLAST

MONDAY MORNING. Edison High School.
I walk through the front gate with
Sully. Classes start in fifteen
minutes.

Something is different.

Everyone is looking at their
phones and smiling.

Then I hear the song we played at
the retirement home, *You Are My
Sunshine*.

Sully takes out his phone and
gets on YouTube.

"Angelo, check this out," he

says. "Somebody posted a video of
us."

I look at his phone.

The people at the retirement home
are smiling and dancing.

I look around at the kids here at
school.

They're smiling, too.

Then I hear another sound.

It's a loud blast that's pure
noise.

It's the Edison *Electro Blast*.

ACKNOWLEDGMENTS

I would like to express my sincere appreciation to everyone who gave me feedback while I was writing this.

COFFEE HOUSE WRITERS GROUP: Cori Amoroso, Leif Beiley, Nicholas Chiazza, Joyce Coffey, Nick Cruz, David Fulps, Monica Gonzales, Richard Guis, Julie Hansen, Amy Haller, Lynne Horne, Steve Hovland, James Jodon, Julie Kim, Paul Kim, Darian Lane, Travis Lee, Patti Mobile, Yusuf Rahman, Charlie Rivers, Jill Rubalcaba, Jay Spring, John Steiner, Jennifer Stilwell, Marilyn Stoner, Stephen Van Fossen, Ron Wolff, Rudra Yamala, Laurie Zupan

GREATER LONG BEACH WRITERS: Leif Beiley, Veronica Cherine, Mary Frances Hill, Donna Nakasone, Moss Sherian

SOCIETY OF CHILDREN'S BOOK WRITERS AND ILLUSTRATORS: Jude Atwood, Christine Henderson, Erin Lagerberg, Debbie Meneses, Shiva Sadeghi, Ava Slocum, Charlotte Van Ryswyk

Thank you, Pam Sheppard, for your advice on creating this series.

Thank you, Laura Perkins, for your feedback and careful editing.

Thank you, Betty Jean, for your patience, your wisdom, and for being my wife.

ABOUT THE AUTHOR

My dream of becoming a writer started at Whitworth College. I was lucky to have a teacher, Dr. Tammy Reid, who believed in me and encouraged me. After college, I began a career as an educator, teaching reading and English at a middle school in Los Angeles. I went to college at night to earn a doctorate in education. I then served as a high school principal and district administrator. One of the most important things I have learned is that everyone can achieve success. Set your sights high, work hard, and never give up. Strive to be the best that you can be.

FINDING FORWARD BOOKS

At Finding Forward Books, we publish short novels for teens about issues faced by teens. Our goal is to help students improve their reading skills, increase their success in school, and develop positive attitudes.

The books are suitable for all teens, including English Learners and students with learning disabilities. They are easy to read, with Lexile measures ranging from 390 to 560.

The books have been praised in Kirkus Reviews, Publishers Weekly BookLife Reviews, Foreword Clarion Reviews, and BlueInk Reviews.

ADDITIONAL TITLES

TAKEN AWAY. A teen learns to cope with life after his dad is sent to prison.

NO PLACE TO HIDE. A discouraged teen improves his reading skills.

NEVER WANTED. A neglected teen is placed in a foster home.

ALL ALONE. A teen learns to deal with his mom's alcoholism.

KNOCKED DOWN. A football player learns the importance of honesty.

OVERSPRAY. A teen experiences grief after his father dies.

TORN. A student with everything
helps a student who has nothing.

BLUE WALL. A troubled teen battles
back from depression.

LETTERZ. A dyslexic teen learns how
to succeed in school.

CANS. A teen who dreams of attending
college struggles against poverty.

FINDING HOME. A homeless teen gets
the help he needs to succeed.

BRADY'S WAY. An insecure teen learns
to think for himself.

STANDING FOR ME. A young adult
strives to succeed in college.

Finding Forward Books

Short Novels for Teens About

Issues Faced by Teens

www.findingforwardbooks.com